Tickling Tigers

Sean Taylor   Jo Brown

ORCHARD BOOKS

Tigers are big and tigers are scary.

Tigers are quick and tigers are hairy.

We climb, we growl, we jump, we chew...

and we're terribly good at tickling too.

So, my cubs, here are my tips
for reaching a creature's ticklish bits.
If you want to make an elephant grin,
tickle the elephant under its chin!

You think that tickling a frog could be funny?
You're right! Try tickling it on its tummy!

To tickle a crocodile, everyone knows,
you find a feather and tickle its nose!

You'll get a giraffe to giggle with glee
if you tickle it lightly behind the knee!

With a gorilla you stay very calm . . .

. . . then tickle it quickly under each arm!

And tickling small tigers
is easy, you know.
You just have to
tickle them
from top
to toe!

But tickling big tigers is never wise!

Big tigers are clever!

They'll take you by surprise!

Big tigers are fierce! And do you know what?

Big tigers aren't ticklish. Not even a jot!

Except for **me!** The tiniest tickle makes me **jiggle** and **giggle** and **wriggle!**

Yes, you see, that's how it's done,
my stripy little bundles of fun.
And there's nothing in the world more snug
than a just-tickled-tiger hug!

For all children who've never
been tickled by a tiger

S.T.

For my two darlings,
Christian and Zazie

J.B.

ORCHARD BOOKS
338 Euston Road, London, NW1 3BH
Orchard Books Australia
17/207 Kent Street, Sydney, NSW 2000

First published in 2010 by Orchard Books

Text © Sean Taylor 2010
Illustrations © Jo Brown 2010

The rights of Sean Taylor to be identified as the author and of Jo Brown
to be identified as the illustrator of this work have been asserted by them in
accordance with the Copyright, Designs and Patents Act, 1988.

A CIP catalogue record for this book is available from the British Library.

ISBN 978 1 84362 951 1

1 3 5 7 9 10 8 6 4 2

Printed in China

Orchard Books is a division of Hachette Children's Books,
an Hachette UK company.

www.hachette.co.uk